# Attitude Adjustment

Attitude Adjustment

Copyright © 2021 BP Books

Published in the United States by BP Books in Tulsa, Oklahoma.

ISBN: 978-1-944918-18-7

For author inquiries please send email to info@bplearning.net.

Bookstore bulk order discounts are available. Please contact info@bplearning.net for more information.

1<sup>st</sup> printing

# Attitude Adjustment

By Alex Azle

# Chapter 1

"Hello. My name is Harwin. I'm with Domestic Servicing," I spoke into the antique gold camera box. It was mounted in a massive white limestone block at the front entry to the home.

"Yes?" returned a woman's voice full of disdain.

I'm used to that. It is beneath most of my clientele to mix with service-industry persons such as myself. Even the 'Certified Disease-Free' staff running the estates, who are themselves service personnel, look down their nose at me.

I pressed ahead in negotiating with the keeper of yet another residential fortress. "I have a service request for um... an A.D.P. 44."

"Oh. That," said the feminine voice, a little less venom present. "Wait there!"

"Very good, Ma'am," I replied using my best, practiced-in-the-mirror for months, smile. Though I wanted to tell her where she could stick her attitude, I wanted more to keep my job.

After a short wait, one half of the twelve-foot-tall black iron doors swung open, revealing a middle-aged man in typical butler's uniform. "Well?" he drawled.

Most customers of this caliber (wealth and paranoia) do not invite me into the house proper. Not after the 2020 pandemic. I am typically conducted to an outbuilding or garage.

The butler raised his eyebrows but offered no further indication that he knew why I was on his master's door step. So, I began again, "Hello Sir. My name is Harwin..."

"I assure you," the butler interrupted, holding up his right hand. "Mrs. Montague has no interest in becoming acquainted. Nor do I."

"Of course, Sir!" I agreed. 'The feeling is mutual you rotten piece of parrot dropping,' I retorted privately.

So there I stood, at the bottom of the grand steps, holding two hard cases full of tools, Mr. Cheerful towering above me at the top. He glanced down at my work boots and then slowly raised his eyes to a point just above my head, causing me to look above. Nodding once he pronounced, "You will be allowed in."

The doorkeeper stepped aside and swept his hand to signal me into the home. With tool cases in hand I quickly mounted the long, curving steps and entered forthwith.

Inside, the entry hall ceiling soared overhead giving the impression of immense space. Which it was!

"This way!" he prompted, catching me with my mouth agape and neck craned to the scene above. There, a 3-D Divinci was moving about on the domed cathedral.

"Very nice," I exclaimed, indicating the motion artwork.

Mr. Cheerful (I never did get his name) rolled his eyes, performed a military about-face and marched off toward an enormous gilt-framed mirror hanging on a side wall.

Somewhat perplexed, I stood, awaiting a cue for where to go, when the looking glass swung out - revealing a hallway.

I hurried to catch up to my usher, leaving the grandness of the entrance cathedral for a narrow side way. It was evident that this access hall was designed and appointed for us - the help.

In short order we emerged within a more 'civilized' area of

the home - a mahogany-paneled, windowless sort of formal con-
versation room. (To hell if I can put a name on all these rooms
the mega-rich have for Lord Nelson knows what!)

The balding, middle-aged butler led me across a thick,
oriental-themed carpet and between two richly-upholstered
couches to the opposite wall. There, making no attempt to dis-
suade me from seeing, he pushed one of the medallions that were
repeated, waist-high, around the room.

The inset wood panel slid sideways, concealing itself in the
wall while revealing a hidden alcove.

"Here!" he said.

A light on the cloister's ceiling flickered to life, casting a sickly
yellow glow in the small space.

And indeed, 'Here' was waiting the A.D.P. 44 for which I had
been called.

"Ah. Yes, Sir," I agreed to his one-word sentence.

The man fixed me with an apprising gaze once again, then
proclaimed, "You will stay here until I personally return for you.
No matter if you have completed your business, you will wait."

"Well, Sir, I have several other service calls to make ..."

"You MUST wait here," he pressed. "You will be personally
awarded beyond and separate whatever your employer pays for
your time."

"Of course, I'll wait. As long as needed!" I exclaimed.

"Very good," he countered.

Moving a step to his right, Mr. Cheerful pointed to a pewter
cigar box atop a heavily carved sideboard.

"If you need more light," he stated.

Taking a more relaxed posture he announced, "I must now
go and receive Mrs. Montague's tea appointments. I will return
as soon as I can."

"Yes, Sir. If you could just tell me what," I began, looking
down at the service bot. "What the little guy is having trouble
about, then I can..."

"I assure you, I truly couldn't say," the butler retorted, making his way back across the oriental carpet before disappearing through a different hidden panel.

Looking around the expansive room, about thirty-feet square, I noticed a complete lack of doors.

'Surely the residents don't use the service corridor,' I wondered.

There were queerer habits of the rich for sure. Many stories I have heard over the years since 'Social Regression' of the twenties. Some tell of tycoons holed-up inside emergency bunkers built within their luxury estates; spending the rest of their existences hiding from the next pandemic. They go on, cut off from the living, afraid to be among the dead.

I pulled the four-foot tall service bot out of his replenishing stall and into the dark-paneled room. This unit was a hard surfaces cleaner and smelled strongly of winterfresh mint. Manufacturers add scent to the various solutions, but when I opened the A.D.P.'s liquid tank a few drips of lavender and lilac glass cleaner told me the odd smell wasn't coming from there.

Wiping a hand across my forehead brought the mint odor close to my eyes, causing them to tear up. There was something pasty and minty on my right hand.

The light in the room was not bright enough for me to work - nor could I see where the goo had originated. From the service bot undoubtedly.

Looking over at the pewter cigar box again, I recalled the rich's penchant for disguising everyday objects - such as doors... and you wouldn't believe what some have done to the loo.

Lifting the silver lid revealed a color touch screen with nine little pictures. Six of the icons I understood, three I did not. The one of a man holding a domed platter must be to summon Mr. Cheerful. There was one with a padlock, one with a violin - neat but not helpful. The one of an open-top box accepting tiny falling money symbols, I couldn't imagine. Rich people!

And one of a window.

No lights.

I tapped the window expecting it to give additional options, instead twelve more window icons appeared.

"What the deuce?" I mumbled while opting for the top-left icon tagged 'SOUTH 1'.

It grew brighter to my left as a section of panel slid down revealing sunlight and glass.

"Ohhhh WINDOW. Right then," I said smiling.

In quick succession all the room's fenestrations were admitting the much-welcomed afternoon sun.

Back at the little service bot I could see now that the optical sensors had all been deliberately slathered with Winterfresh Mint Extra-Whitening Dentagleam.

'Now what in Lord Snedington's Court would,' was running through my head when a shadow passed across my four-foot friend, startling me.

Embarrassed, I turned around - as if to get a tool from my open case.

Standing a few yards behind me was a woman of ninety plus years, hunched over a designer cane, dressed in a purple bathrobe.

"Hello!" I offered cheerily. "Just here to get this little fella cleaned up and back in action."

The robe-wearing senior was glaring daggers at the service bot. Then her eyes lifted and locked on mine as I gave my best practiced smile. She returned my smile, hers as wide as the Thames, showing off a perfect mouth of brilliant white ceramic teeth; the kind of teeth that one would polish with Winterfresh Mint Extra-Whitening Dentagleam.

Just as I tipped my hat to the lady, she threw her head back and let out a wicked cackle. Turning, she made her way to another hidden doorway and before leaving, flipped me the middle finger adding one final shriek.

"Well, I've seen it all," said I to myself.

And if it had been 'ALL' that I'd witnessed over the years then I wouldn't be preparing this narrative for my barrister.

# Chapter 2

Three more times that month I had to make the same service call. Three more times the only problem was Dentagleam covering the unit's optics. And so it was an easy extra five hundred in my pocket to do as Mr. Cheerful required. If I had let it go at that, the situation wouldn't look quite so dire... but I'm getting ahead of myself. Let me first explain a bit of background before I lay out my defense.

My brother is a top designer for the leading armech maker in Seoul. TG-50's and MM-84's, you know, front-line and front-page battle-mechs. I didn't want to be a part of 'The Weaponization of Things' when we both chose our career paths. But he's playing with top-of-the-line hardware. And my cousin, the same age as myself, she's a project manager for Exomine. Yes. "That" Exomine. The one that just hauled in a four-hundred ton space rock rich in platinum, gold, tungsten... all kinds of rare-earths. She gets a percentage of that find.

Eventually I came to the realization that my ranking in the cyber-technology hierarchy is lower than the recycling and refuse processing robots (and their human counterparts). I've lost my enthusiasm for the job... and life in general.

As I said earlier, if the old woman's treatment of service bots, or respect for their technicians, was an isolated incident - the situation might be different.

Not by any measure (English or Metric) was it an isolated incident.

One of my first house calls was not to the rich, in fact the customer may have been my equal as far as income standards. It was their lack of basic sanitation I found deplorable.

As the post-pandemic market for DSB's... Oh sorry. That's what we call Domestic Service Robots in the business. As the market boomed it was an exciting time to be in Applied AI. Extensive knowledge of software wasn't needed - though a level of bravery was. You simply couldn't know of diseases the customer might harbor. But we were paid well for the first few boom years - until capable installers caught up to the exponential demand.

This particular job was at least fifteen years back, and it started off regular-like.

My mobile beeped with an install assignment for one of Domestic Servicing's basic sanitation models. I first stopped by our self-serve warehouse to pick up the unit and its accompanying parts: docking station, plumbing kit, electrical conduit and a retro-fit cabinet concealer to house it all.

When Get-R-Done (that's the model name of my Ford work van) turned us onto the customer's street I should have called in sick, but I was young and could only think of the good money.

Honestly, the particular house didn't look at all worse than any other in the area: crushed rock with all manner of weeds sprouting through for a yard, a little bit of brick on the front (these houses were over a century old), peeling wood siding and curling asphalt shingles of the cheapest grade. Some even had chimneys and ALL of them had junk of one type or another proudly displayed on the front porch (or waiting on the side of the house for its day out front).

Pulling into the cracked driveway of 310 South Archer I

grabbed my measure-all and headed for the customer's aluminum front door. Tapping on the glass first, I waited with the rusted-out refrigerator that had stained the Astro-turf carpet upon which we both stood.

"COME IN!" a raspy, older woman by the sound of it returned from the unseen interior.

Before I could reply, the glass in the door, and my teeth, rattled as a Boeing Super 900 screamed to gain altitude, having just lifted off the runway at TIA, half a mile behind me. Loving aircraft since childhood, I turned around to watch the world's largest jetliner fly just above the neighboring rooftops. When I turned back, a man of fifty or so (it was hard to tell at my age of twenty-four) opened the screen door and was awaiting my entry.

"Howdy! You the robot man I guess we called."

"I am, Sir," I said with pride. This was back when the excitement of the technology filled my head.

"Come on in 'ere, then. My name's Nigel... and this is my mother," he said, indicating the mostly toothless woman sitting on one of those wheeled walkers, with handle bars and a padded board.

In response, the woman lifted her white can of discount beer and warmly offered, "Hi there!"

Just inside the front door, the three of us were in the combined entryway, parlor and dining room - being a small featureless white box - which held no furniture.

"In here is where we were thinkin' of puttin' the thing," Nigel drawled, leading the way into a small kitchen. The cabinets formed a typical 'U' shaped eatery wherein sat a folding-leg card table. Around this wobbly excuse were several outdoor plastic chairs and the space's electric icebox. Topping the table was a large glass ashtray encircled by fifteen empty beer cans.

Pushing out one chair with his foot to indicate I could sit, Nigel took the remaining seat opposite me. Once seated at the kitchen 'table' he leaned sideways, pulled open the refrigerator door, grabbed two pints of ale and offered me one in the process.

"Here I come, Junior!" Mom called out, still seated in the walker, her slippered feet working to get the conveyance to the empty place at the table.

As I was on business, I declined the offered refreshment. The beverage went to Mom, who I discovered, as much as I tried not to, was bra-less under her white tank top.

But more than Mom's attire, what concerned me was the strong odor of cat urine. I was worried they would return the DSB when they, as many others had, discovered that domestic robots and pets do not cohabitate willingly. Some dogs get over it, as I am sure you've heard, but cats almost always move out. I've had more than one customer accuse the service bot of actually consuming the family cat. Of course this is utter nonsense or, I should say that NONE of the units ship from the factory with that possibility anywhere in their protocols.

Protocols can be altered.

"What's 'ees name?" asked Mom, lighting an actual tobacco cigarette.

"Why, my name is Harwin, ma'am. My apologies for not introducing myself proper."

Setting his beer can down, Nigel pointed out that Mom was actually asking about the DSB they'd purchased. "She's got plans for 'eem," drawled Nigel, giving me a knowing wink.

Trying not to imagine what ANY of those plans might be, I blurted out, "He's a Basic Operations Iteration 2."

The aging woman considered this for a moment, puffing thoughtfully on a Pall Mall, then asked, "Can I call 'eem 'Boy'?"

My eyes grew large with shock. I have been living here my whole life and have heard some racist things, but never so direct. WE believe ourselves to be the 'World's City'.

Nigel quickly explained, "She didn't mean it like that!"

To his mother he stated, "We can do that later. The webplace said we can name 'eem as we want, Ma."

In reply, Mom held up her empty beer can and shook it about.

"That's correct, Sir. Completely customizable user settings," I said, recovering my professional demeanor.

Pointing over my left shoulder, Nigel stated, "We really think he should live right...char."

Behind me was a cavity left behind by a defunct (and waiting on the side of the house) wall oven.

"Hmm," I grunted, rising from my chair and pulling my measure-all from my belt. Kneeling on the linoleum floor, left over from the last century, I leaned into the opening of the cabinet to set the measure-all in the approximate center. As I prepared to push the scan button, something above me caught my eye. Quickly, I ducked back, took a sharp breath and stood in one swift, fluid motion.

Nigel was there before I even had the word 'roach' out of my mouth, swinging a fly-swatter, yelling with each strike.

Grabbing her son's unattended pint, Mom stated, "They're so hard to get rid of. The cats do a decent enough job at it though."

Indeed, during a trip out to my van for tools, one of the cats chased a roach across the furniture-deficient 'entry' room and with a final pounce, caught the pest.

I finished the install. I feel it important to tell you that, because a number of times, when a roach crawled over my hand or dropped into my hair, I almost quit. Not just the install, but the Company as well.

While working inside kitchen cabinets running hot water, a drain line and an electrical extension, it was necessary to blame the Company for sending me to that job. Needing to maintain courtesy with the customer, I silently cursed my employer.

It worked.

# Chapter 3

The majority of my customers were much more affluent... and much more paranoid about communicable diseases.

As much as the technology was ready, the skyrocketing demand for my services was a result of two things. The combination of both formed the knock-out punch that brought DSB's to every home, business, theme park, church and even warehouse that could afford them.

First was an insatiable desire for homes and businesses to be sanitized multiple times per day.

Second was the desire for the former plus the wish to limit exposure to cleaning service personnel. Compounding the issue would be the excessive labor costs inherent to achieving society's new standards.

Enter: Domestic Service Robots.

The highest quality DSB's are Japanese, German and Korean. Very expensive. A Krupp's Basic you could trade for an Italian sports car. Those are commercial models. I've dealt in a few, but not really my area of the market.

The more affordable, yet effective, units come from American designers* (America doesn't MAKE anything) and the Chinese

- which garner over half the market.

The rest are junk... and thanks to our most excellent Creator in heaven, my company doesn't carry them.

Throughout my career I have at least had the good fortune of providing and representing quality hardware. This next and final customer ordered the highest quality DSB from Domestic Servicing.

It all came to a head about a month back.

I have not worked since.

Though everything culminated a month ago, the job that brought me to that infamous end began four months previous.

It was a typical enough start - my mobile blaring 'Taking Care of Business' at me, signaling a new job order. The address was south Baldwin, which meant mega-money. In this neighborhood it is now the trend to snap up three or more estates worth ten million each, knock them down and build a monstrosity costing hundreds of millions.

The order was for a GG-IV, top of the line, placed by one Martin Zift.

'Where have I heard that name?' I pondered while Get-R-Done drove us to the warehouse.

I was in back, checking over the parts bins, when it hit me like a pint of Watley's Red Barrel. The customer, Zift, was a newer multi-billionaire. He had made it all as a result of humanity's fear after the COVID-19 event. According to NBBC (No-Bull Biography Channel), he 'pioneered' a priority healthcare insurance policy.

A person in possession of this elite policy is guaranteed priority, no-wait access to a select group of the best hospitals in the event of a public health crisis. Policy holders have first pick of everything - and many things are stockpiled in private store rooms that Zift's company set up in the hospitals.

When asked about the ethics of such a caste system within healthcare, the hospitals were quick to point out that the money they were receiving now from the Zift-policies was treating large numbers of poor people today and tomorrow. Not many politicians have had the desire to challenge the scheme - they and their family members are all discounted policy holders.

As I recalled his biography, still in the back looking over my tools, Get-R-Done pulled up to the warehouse nose forward. Again! There is no way to 'SAVE' if you want the thing to park forward or backwise. It will keep 999 music stations - but not if you want the bonnet or the boot to go first.

"Vehicle input command! Back your rear to the building!" I yelled to the green eye set above the van's center screen.

While we repositioned I looked over the job specifics on my mobile - and that's when I saw that this was NOT going to be a typical install.

Next to the model GG-IV, within the quantity box, was the number '20'.

I thought it a mistake and decided to read the entire work order - including the contract. As this would take some time I hopped up front, pulled the document up on Get-R-Done's large screen, then tinted the windows to their utmost.

In short, the quantity of units purchased was spot-on.

Zift had placed, confirmed and pre-paid for the largest single order Domestic Servicing had ever received.

With eighteen years of experience I was the most trusted installer. The contract stated that only one installer could be sent and that it must be the company's best installer. Thus, where a team would be ideal, I went alone.

But first I had to figure out how to get twenty GG-IV's, which are twice the size of a person, into my van. There simply wasn't that much room, so I had to get permission from Sid, he's Operation's Chief, to use four additional vans that were parked at our warehouse.

All loaded and a half hour's trip to the wealthy side of town found my caravan in front of wrought-iron gates adorned with an enormous golden 'Z'.

Martin Zift's automated sentry program greeted me by way of requesting access to Get-R-Done's computer. It also posed some verbal security and health questions to me.

While talking 'nice' to me, the sentry was using high-order decryption tactics to try to enter the five vans' and my mobile's secure files. Only the fact that my brother had given me an ultra-secure Korean OS for personal use kept my info safe. My advanced operating system had come in handy in the past (and would do so again).

When the decorative gates parted we entered an artificial canyon of high brick walls. The cobblestone drive curved, keeping what lay ahead concealed. Half a mile in, our progress was halted by a solid-steel blockade, with guardhouses on each side. Here the sentry program ordered me to exit my van, then enter the (empty) hut on the right, and receive further instructions.

I complied, but not before throwing the kill-switch to Get-R-Done's onboard computer. An invasive sweep of all the vans was to follow, and the guard shack, built as a miniature Swiss Chalet, was designed (hopefully) to shield me from intense, probing radiation.

The follow-on vans would be vulnerable to intrusion for a split second as they rebooted after shutting down due to the radiation spike. Mine would remain safe.

Satisfied, the sentry lowered the blast shield into the earth, granting me entry to the paradise that hundreds of billions could provide.

I would have stopped at the three-story expanse of stone and timber had Get-R-Done not received specific directions; I later learned that structure to be the garage.

We eventually came to a massive chateau, probably larger than its Swiss counterpart, circumnavigated a bronze statue in the roundabout and parked, all the vans lined in a precise row.

Emerging from my vehicle I was immediately confronted

by four identical personal-assistant robots. With an electronic wheeze, they warned, "Submit! You are trespassing and will be escorted off premises without delay!"

The units, shaped like humanoids, made to encircle me but were too slow. All four personal assistants, with their ill-fitting assignment to security detail, hobbled about trying miserably to subdue me.

Three times we had gone around the parked vans when a high, nasal voice called out, "HALT! Halt you imbeciles!"

While the four robots took a few more faltering steps, their servos whining as they stood up straight, I froze in place, concerned that whoever had made the demand might have had a weapon.

From my left, previously concealed behind the statue, appeared a short man, some fifty-odd years of age. Shorter than his statue conveyed, for it was an idealized replica of himself, Martin Zift had black curly hair, gold-rim glasses and was decked out in a flamboyant Hawaiian shirt.

With a Command-It whole-house controller strapped to one wrist, Zift came right up to me, ranting and flailing his arms, "Useless! Utterly and woefully useless machines!"

Straightening while turning toward him, I cheerily greeted, "Good morning, Sir! My name is Harwin and I am here from Domestic Servicing."

"Of course you are!" Mr. Zift swiftly countered. "You've been employed there for eighteen years. Prior to that you attended Zurich Institute of Technology. You live alone, unless you count all the robots, and... your favorite eatery is Jippies."

I've encountered more interesting introductions, although the details supplied are usually about the other person.

"Ah. Yes Sir."

Turning his wrist so I could read my name on the screen of his Command-It, he continued, "There are 125 other interesting tidbits, plus thousands of minor details, about one Harwin B.

Sartain from Brighton, but none that interest me more than the fact that you are the brother of Leland E. Sartain."

'My brother?'

Not sure how to respond, I stood there in a fashion equaling a simpleton out of his depth.

Zift frowned up at me. After an awkward silence he asked, "Why didn't you go into defense with your brother? So much more lucrative!"

To this I gave my honest answer. "Well, Sir, I didn't want to weaponize the planet."

"Bah!" he spat. "Someone else will just take your place. Might as well get over it and get paid."

"I am over it. Now. But years ago I guess..."

My boisterous and very forward customer clapped both of my shoulders with each word, "Catch. Up. Or. Die. Off."

This truly startled me. In polite society, one absolutely adhered to the government adverts that stated, "Two persons means two meters..."

Shaken, I asked, "You're not... not concerned about a contagion?"

Smiling up at me, still holding my shoulders, Martin Zift shook his head and stated, "Not a bit! And neither are you, Harwin. Besides, it is an overblown, hyped-up tactic used to exploit the sheeple!"

"But, you, pioneered... " I blubbered.

"Really Harwin," he whined with disappointment. "I assumed too highly of you perchance?"

"Oh, no, Sir! My apologies, Sir. I am intensely loyal to our customers and committed to the highest level of service!"

"Yes! Yes!" Zift proclaimed in a nasal tone. "Then you will have NO problem carrying out my wishes for the duration of the job?"

This was an order in the form of a question; something the rich and powerful employ exhaustingly and one to which I am accustomed. But I was not fully immune to the effect with which it could be wielded.

Zift is a master at personal manipulation - that much had just been proven at our introduction. But with such wealth added to his ability - it was hard to resist.

At first I agreed to all his eccentric, and well paid for, demands.

Standing under a soaring stone archway of the home's front portico, Martin Zift outlined his requirements.

Stipulation One: I must stay within his estate's walls until job completion. To placate my unease Zift personally showed me to a suite on the fifth floor, one that Vegas Whales would find impressive.

Stipulation Two: I would sign a non-disclosure and privacy document to never divulge anything about his property, buildings or other structures, nor would I discuss ANY generalities or details about the install I was about to perform.

# Chapter 4

Over a meal delivered exclusively by 'The Four Stooges', (the personal-assistant robots), I began to understand what Zift really wanted and why he had chosen me specifically to provide for his wishes.

After the prime rib stuffed with crème-crab, he began whining about keeping the roaches out. I'm embarrassed to admit now, but I was wholly relieved upon discerning that Zift was referring to his fellow citizens... and not the cupboard-creeps I had come to abhor.

Zift was paranoid, not of disease but of the public at large. Apparently his money did not guarantee a peaceful existence. He ranted that after some 'ordeal' with his hired security personnel, Zift up and fired all of them, vowing to find obedient replacements. Scared of betrayal, he rarely allowed visitors. No human 'help' did I ever witness. The estate employed an automated garage with secure docks for all ground deliveries, where an army of specific-task robots would take over goods disbursement and storage. All of his meals arrived by courier and then were bot-delivered to one of nineteen 'dining theaters' around the vast estate. My favorite was a reproduction of a Venice water-side cafe (with actual gondolas!).

Because of protestors, violent letters and paint-slinging activists at his offices, Zift built his mega-estate as a refuge. But without security to tackle the occasional crazy that found their way in, he was left exposed.

"It's not my fault they're too poor! Those people are the bacteria on my backside," he commented. "And I don't control the market rates of healthcare."

Between bites I would nod in agreement with my ranting dinner host. I didn't agree with most of what he said but he was going to pay me very generously, plus it seemed the cordial behavior the exquisite meal deserved.

"They're awful, Sir. Right wicked!" I concurred.

His oration eventually recalled the attempt his personal-assistant robots made at subduing me.

"Well, Sir," I replied wiping my mouth with a satin napkin. "Those units were never intended to be as agile or responsive as human reflexes."

Throwing his napkin down onto our sixth, no - it was the seventh course, lobster bisque with Cajun sausage, Zift angrily retorted, "Then where the hell can I get a unit capable of taking down a man?"

His question set my mind awhirl about legalities, special permits, advanced threat assessment, autonomy software protocols... There was only one answer, "It would have to be a military armech. But I don't think," I stated cautiously. "I'm not sure even YOU could get the proper clearances..."

Zift held up both hands to stop me. "Not the software needed. NOT the government licensing. But the physical capability to pursue and apprehend a grown, athletic man."

Frowning in thought, I haltingly listed the types of robots that might fit the bill, "A perimeter patroller - but those are too big and clumsy. Maybe a modified general-cleaning model. Or a floor... no, too weak. Ah," I said thinking of a specialized unit. "A grounds keeping..."

I stopped mid-sentence, my mouth forming a perfect 'O', as the proverbial light bulb kicked on. The face of my dinner host lit with a smile, for he had just purchased twenty of the most versatile, advanced robotic grounds keeping units available.

He touted, "They even come with built-in weapons!" With a short laugh he added, "All they need is a little attitude adjustment."

Lying awake in bed that first night forced the question: Could I go through with Martin Zift's plan to weaponize, no - that's not accurate, they already had weapons... Would I, or should I, "militarize" a domestic grass-clipping, hedge-mending, topiary-tending robot?

Before I answer that question, allow me to tell of some weird, humorous and downright disturbing service calls I've answered over the past eighteen years.

More than a few DSB's have I seen made up in women's clothing, cosmetics and all - had to clean the optics and audio interface for most.

Many children like to ride around on our popular Oscar model - early replacement of wheel bearings for those units.

Ill-tempered canines tear off the rubber parts - standard gel-patches there.

I have pulled several units from swimming pools, requiring total replacement. 'It's a robot, not a superhero!'

One DSB I shoveled out of a fireplace. That story still doesn't add up.

Several have been run over by people playing 'driver', of which they were ticketed for operating a motor vehicle.

At the home of one bow-hunting customer, the lawn-bot required new servos and sixteen hot-weld patches to its polycarbonate body. "Great target practice!" he insisted.

And many of us have heard of Ki-Ki, the gorilla at the Beijing

Zoo, taking its habitat sanitation unit for a mate. The zoologist thought it best to encase the bot in fur - to keep Ki-Ki from becoming agitated by a machine.

But Zift's situation was by far the most extreme.

After a few hours of restless soul-searching I came to the realization, and resolution, that Zift could afford to pay me more for what he was wanting.

And so he did!

Thus I was happy to deliver.

Zift had used my public data points to generate a fairly spot-on personality assessment of me.

Oh, I'm not naive. I know he paid for all my private info as well. He took a gamble, no doubt. I might have refused at any point and marched to the authorities with his crazy idea, but it would have been my word against his.

Zift researched several people's bios, going back decades. From the list of candidates (he never told me the names), I was selected. He knew that I had purchased programming tutorials fifteen years ago, teaching myself software design. That he mentioned the work my brother did in Korea told me he was betting that I had learned some special skills from my sibling. Well, I certainly had.

His initial scan of my systems at his front gate told him that I had progressed beyond 'corporate programmer'. How far? He wouldn't find out until seventy-seven days after I had completed the job for him.

That particular number of days landed on the twenty-fifth anniversary of his first insurance policy offering and as such, so I learned over the course of my stay, Mr. Zift would be having his top executives and elite policy holders out to his estate for a celebration.

In order for me to deliver the level of technical accuracy the job required, Zift had to grant me unprecedented access to his home's sentry program, aptly named 'Q'. Absolutely imperative was it that the lethal yardmen be precisely integrated with Q; otherwise, an admitted visitor might receive a topiary haircut or experience a limb-lopping.

Working while Zift watched over my shoulder was nothing short of maddening. At first I wasn't sure if I would be able to pull off my surprise for his upcoming party. The man was an amateur programmer and knew his home's systems fairly well. However, the new units HAD to be programmed using my special operating system, and that I could do from my mobile at night.

Eventually, I worked out how to spoof the sentry program by writing a host of alterations and additions into the grounds keeper's software and disguising it as a 'core motor-control routine,' which opened a back door into Q. This kept Zift and Q from even questioning its content.

When the big day arrived I was long gone from Martin Zift's employment.

Also 'Gone' was that last hint of respect for the customer - and most of humanity. Their sordid and perverted uses of my electro-mechanical friends had finally broken me.

# Chapter 5

On the twenty-fifth anniversary of Zift's first insurance policy offering, during the height of his private party, 'Operation Attitude Adjustment' launched.

The first 'attitude' adjusted was Q's. Temporarily replaced was his suspect and thorough demeanor for one of acceptance and cordiality.

With this new sunnier outlook Q sent invitations to every mobile in a thirty mile radius to, "Come one, come all to a special 'Thanks to the community' event at Zift Manor. The first 1000 persons to shake Mr. Zift's hand will receive a free Saynex Holo-Pro Plus!"

This assured a wave of pressing, insisting, suffocating humanity would quickly and thoroughly confuse things all over the property - most importantly distracting Zift.

I really would have liked to take control of Q from a remote location in order to counter anything my former employer might do to thwart my scheme - alas it couldn't be done. Everything had to be programmed during my stay at the estate; his system was very insulated from outside influence.

Evite sent, Q instructed the newcomers to park at a variety of "preferred" locations, and thus guided them to the cricket pitch, cobbled garden paths, the rear terrace and all around Zift's original guest's luxury autos, blocking their exit.

Disabled were ALL forms of communication, except those of Q and the estate's rogue robots. The satellite uplinks, net connections, mobiles and RF signals were all blocked. With the estate's private cellular network Q continued to orchestrate the movement of newcomers while routing all outbound communication attempts to an unhelpful comsbot.

This kept the "guests" ability to interfere with the follow-on phases to a minimum, albeit they were undoubtedly frustrated at the connective-isolation.

With arrivals jamming the brick-canyon entry drive phase two, or "Fun on the Run," began in earnest. The groundskeeper assault bots exchanged their disdain of human trespassers for that of automobiles.

They torched every vehicle, starting at the outer perimeter of the estate and working toward the center. This way, when the smoke and fires alerted all in attendance that the party was over, they were trapped by burning wreckage. This compounded the fear and chaos during my "friends" protracted campaign of destruction.

Utilizing the features with my Korean battle ware, I provided the [confidential] vehicle manufacturers maintenance codes to the altered groundskeepers. To use them, the automobile hunters simply had to get within about twenty meters and transmit overload instructions to the battery banks. The instantaneous power surge turned the ampacitors into mini-stars, something only ever witnessed in extreme laboratory destructive testing.

For the few gasoline custom-rods that Zift's mega-rich friends favored, a quick reach under the vehicle to slash into the gas tank did the trick. (There's news video of a groundskeeper holding its gasoline-splashed, flaming chainsaw over its head while making its way from one target to the next. The damn news media ran this on repeat for three days.)

As hundreds of vehicle fires blazed the groundskeeper assault bots received instructions of which Zift himself would be proud. The mechanized maniacs then instigated a campaign to "eject all humans" from the premises. This had unintended consequences. Some people were trampled in the human stampede which came from the realization that they were now being pursued. Others fell or were crushed against decorative concrete garden walls in the panic to flee.

Adding to this madness, Zift was screaming, "They'll kill us all!"

I really had thought that the precautions and specific instructions I had given would see all the people unharmed. The bots were coded to restrict all use of their gardening implements against humans and animals but they could still grab, grip, grapple and pull, as well as pursue all trespassers - meaning everyone. Pursue they DID!

I misjudged, or failed to consider, that humans tire before robots. Tragically (a qualifying word my barrister advised me to use) a number of people were captured then dragged by hair, feet, arms and clothing to the front gate, a considerable distance. There the bloody and broken corpses were left with the stern warning to: "Cease all attempts of re-entry onto Zift properties!"

He (my barrister) is hopeful that I could receive a lesser charge of 'accidental death' instead of the forty-two 'wilful murder' counts against me.

Looking back, while I was conceiving my plan, I believed that Martin Zift would bear much of the blame. After all, I was only trying to 'placate a madman's requests, satisfy the Company's obligations to its customer while attempting to create a safe yet effective means of securing personal property.'

This is our official press release statement, you're undoubtedly tired of seeing it scroll past under my police photo every time you turn on the telly.

Using Zift as a partial or complete scapegoat is next to impossible now. They located Zift sure enough, his left leg and most of his head anyhow, underneath the bayou boardwalk of his crocodile habitat. Seems the African beasts knew their captor well and were eager to repay his kindness.

The electro-shock barrier was cut during the general destruction which all of the DSB's took part in during the final phase at Zift Manor.

I hadn't ordered the felling of specific fences, outbuildings and the like - that would have taken too long for me to specifically code. The targets were listed by size and shape. Anything taller than seven feet (this was intended to absolutely safeguard humans) and straight within one inch over a six foot length, was open to demolition.

Not much is left standing. Q removed the prohibition on using chainsaws, grass-lasers, loppers and brute force. The mega-garage was already engulfed in flames by this point. I read somewhere that several of Zift's World War Two era Army trucks held several hundred liters of petrol and had been targeted earlier during the vehicle rampage of phase two. The police were helpless. Six hours after it began, an anti-terrorist commando team was called in to halt the hacked yard men.

Days after my arrest 3N (News Now Network) had headlined my story as the "New Global Cyber Pandemic" with the subheading of, "No longer safe in our own homes." There was news video of panic and paranoia. People were banishing their DSB's to the back porch if not the rubbish heap. Stories of demonic possession emerged - undoubtedly planted by anti-technologists - but the Networks ran them!

"I'm buggered!" I exclaimed upon seeing the news.

I verily underestimated how dependent we had all become on the Domestic Service Robot. In only three decades following COVID-19 there are now more DSB's on Earth than people. By comparison, that is faster than the adoption of the internet.

I had only affected some one-hundred and seventy robots, all of these Zift's. And I did NOT use a virus, thus my handiwork couldn't spread.

But what I did accomplish - not on purpose - was to destroy consumer confidence in autonomous systems and devices.

The prosecution has laid additional charges on behalf of the 'citizenry-at-large' for compensatory damages for anyone needing therapy due to mental anguish I may have caused.

"Great Marley's ghost!" my barrister mumbled upon hearing this latest charge.

When he met my distressed and questioning gaze he whispered, "That one's reserved for big corporations. Never heard it used against an individual."

Citing that my actions had caused the technology-heavy stock market to dip twenty percent, the prosecutor recommended I be held without bond.

The magistrate scowled then offered, "Yes. My retirement portfolio has taken it even worse. BOND WITHHELD!"

When I objected with an outburst of colorful metaphors, he rapped his wooden gavel at me and sneered, "You've a terrible attitude, young man, and I have just the thing to adjust it..."